CHAPTER

ONE

...not gonna lie, speeding through a busy city chasing bad guys while trying not to fly into a wall—yeah, I've been Spider-Man for nearly a year, and I'm *still* getting used to it.

But, okay, I admit it—mainly, it's freaking awesome!

Spider-Man Threat or Menace?

The Daily Bugle
We don't give a pass just because they have a mask

Printing the truth since 1898

Number two: Are you somehow related to that other Spider-Man in Queens?

SENT!

SW!PE

No. We're not cousins or long-lost bros reunited. Peter Parker and I aren't family. But...

...we *are* friends, and Peter's super cool about supporting me.

SW!PE

morales1610: My Brother from Another

And, IDK, it's sorta nice to have someone nearby who just gets it, you know?

Also, and I *swear* I'm not humblebragging, I have a couple of cool super-powers that Peter admits make him drool.

Yo, Spider-Man, say something for the 'Gram, bro!

I'm *not* your gram, *bro!*

For example, I can...

Have a good day, Spider-Man.

...make myself invisible!

OMG! Yo, did you see that?! He disappeared!

OMG! Oh man, I wasn't recording!

Which, c'mon, will camouflage ever get old?

And I can stun bad guys with my VENOM BLAST! Which is awesome, for sure, but I *mainly* use it as a last resort.

Something tells me those guys *aren't* museum employees.

BROOKLYN MUSEUM TRANSPORT

What does a super hero do when they're not saving the world?

Well...

Wait, so is it *whoa*, then *mop*, and then—

No, no, Miles, it's *mop* first, **then** you hit the *whoa*...

Ugh. How are you doing this so easily, Ganke?

While you're busy fighting bad guys, I'm busy getting my dance on, obviously.

Okay, I think I got it this time... I'm doing it, I'm doing—

Ummm...

Okay, so I'm not doing it. *Welp.*

Cheer up, bro. You may have a twenty-three rating in **dancing ability,** but you're, like, a ninety-nine in **kick butt**.

Uh-oh. My spidey-sense is buzzing. Something's up...

Uhh, Ganke, I gotta go, man!

Oh snap, that's your *it's about to get real* face. Be safe, bro! Later!

8

The Rene-**what?**

It's a dance. Kinda goes like... You know what? Forget it.

Peter Parker claims my aim will improve with more experience, but so far it still kinda...sucks, TBH.

Looks like you two are already tied up.

KLINK

See, this is why I never leave home without bug spray!

Trinity, **less** witty banter and **more** escape plan, yeah?

COUGH COUGH

Sorry, man, but you heard Vex—we've gotta fly.

Enjoy your **solo** dance party!

Keep up, Vex!

You serious right now? You know I hate heights!

Hang gliders in backpacks? That's fun.

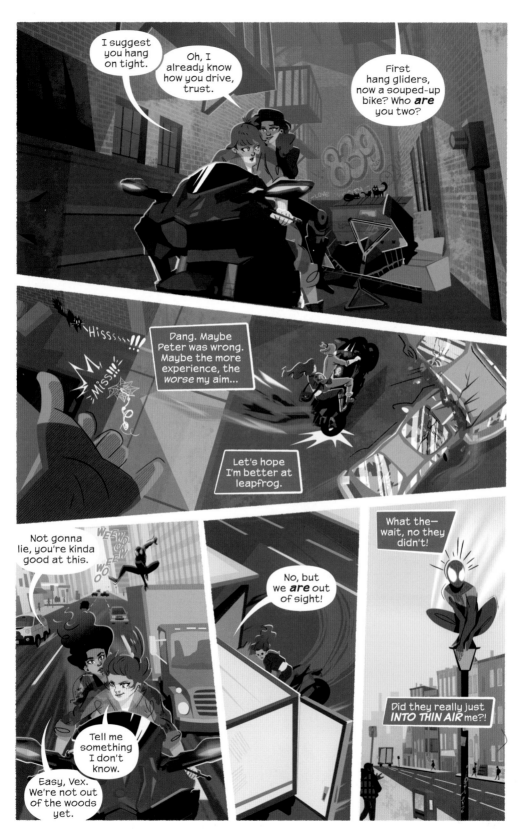

11

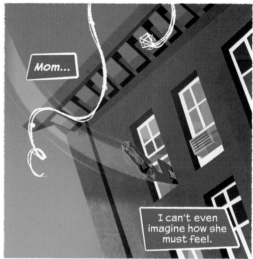

I love you too, Camila. Please be careful, hermana, okay?

What'd your sister say, Rio? Everyone okay?

Click

The house I grew up in. Where your Tía Camila lives now.

Look.

Thankfully, everyone's mostly okay, but they've lost nearly everything.

What about the house?

What house?

You remember now, mijo?

That's my favorite climbing tree. Wow, it was huge even way back when you were a kid.

Cuidado, mijo.

"So many great memories there. My quinceañera.

"My first kiss."

No offense, but *EWWWW*. Like, seriously, that's gross.

"The first time you took me home, we carved our initials in that tree—you remember, baby?"

"Sí, mi amor, how could I forget?

"But I'm afraid now it's..."

But what about the new easel you've been saving for?

My old easel is just fine. I want to help.

Proud of you, son.

I just wish I could do more.

There has to be a way to raise relief money quickly.

Wait... I know what we can do!

Beth's

The next day. Saturday.

Fundraiser block party for Puerto Rico!

I'll take one!

Miles
Fundraiser Block Party for Puerto Rico! Details below:

Kamala - I'm in!

Doreen - Me too!

Ganke - Don't forget meeeeeee!

17

The next evening.

You should've seen your Tía Camila's face when she finally found me in that tree, Miles. Her cheeks matched the flowers, and she...

SCRIBBLE SCRIBBLE

Mijo, are you feeling well? You seem...elsewhere. If you don't want to hear me talk about growing up in Puerto Rico, it's okay, but...

Plus, you haven't touched your pork chop.

Huh? What? No, your story's great, Mom. Really fascinating, yeah.

BZZZ BZZ BZZ

And, Dad, these pork chops are...are... an interesting texture.

BZZZ BZZZ BZZ

Hey, man, are you on your way back to school yet?

Nope. It's Sunday. Family Dinner.

Wait, no phones at the table!

GANKE

Don't disrespect family dinner, bro!

Make sure you bring me a plate of whatever deliciousness your mom made!

Dad cooked tonight...
(˘ ﹏ ˘) ｡˚ ⋆｡˚ ✧*(>д<)*˚⋆

Nooooo! NEVER MIND!!
(╯︵╰,) (╯︵╰,)

Grrr... These knives must need resharpening!

Well, I was just saying that your abuela used to—

I'm sorry, guys.

But if I wanna get an early start tomorrow passing out flyers on campus, I should head out now.

CHAPTER

TWO

The next day.

Kyle, will you **at least** let me take your suitcase to your room?

Thanks for the ride, Dad.

While you're at boarding school, who's gonna watch the Buckeyes with me?

Umm, me. I'll be home every weekend. Football Saturdays live on!

BROOKLYN VISIONS ACADEMY

You're invited to a special disaster relief fundraiser! It's for—

The earthquakes in Puerto Rico.

Oh, this is awesome.

May I have one too?

This is outstanding. What's your name, young man?

Miles, sir. Miles Morales.

Well, Miles. You can count on our family's support— right, Kyle?

Definitely!

Do you go to school here too? I've never seen you around.

Yeah, we just moved here from Cleveland. Today's my first day.

Maybe Miles can show you around today?

DAD.

I'm sorry, Miles. I'm sure you have your own stuff going on and—

I don't have anything going on. I mean, uh, I'm cool with it if you are.

Yeah? You sure?

It's settled, then. Thanks, Miles. And I'm gonna show your flyer to my boss. Maybe he'd consider sponsoring it.

That would be great!

Okay, so what's your first class?

Um, looks like art.

Me too. Sweet.

Oh wow, your work is incredible.

Thanks! Yours too.

I thought so...until I saw yours.

Haha, no way. Let's just agree we're **both** talented, yeah?

Kyle, this is absolutely brilliant color work. Miles just asked me last week how he could improve his coloring. Maybe you could offer him a few suggestions?

Umm, sure. If that's what Miles wants?

Yeah, well, maybe we could get together one day after school? You could show me how you get those shadows to stretch like that.

BRRAWGGGGG

Yeah, uh, that's... cool...with me... thanks.

Yeah, sure. Maybe.

ZZZIPPPP ZIPP

Hey, K. Tell your new friend my boss not only wants to sponsor the fundraiser, he'll also fly donations to Puerto Rico on his personal jet. And I even convinced him to include an art contest because I knew you'd love that. Basically, there'll be a small entry fee, and he'll make a big show of buying the winning piece for a big donation, and it'll all go to the relief fund. Anyway, Mom and I are proud and appreciative of how you've handled this move. Love you!

From my dad...

10-4. Thanks, dispatch.

ARGHGHGH!

Everything okay over there, roomie?

TECH TIMES

I'm the worst artist who ever lived. But yeah, couldn't be better.

I know you artist types are sensitive about your work, but you're putting way too much pressure on yourself. You gotta—

I take it you're going out?

Calling all units, we've got a 211 in progress. Suspect is headed north up Broadway. Suspect is female, late teens, red hair, on a motorcycle and...

Might as well. It's not like I'm doing anything else important.

Bro, after you're finished making New York safe again, we should talk about hanging up your clothes when—

Your friend is about to risk his life to make this world a better place and *his jeans* are what you're worried about?

Hey, all I'm asking is for a teensy bit of roommate consideration ...but yeah, be safe!

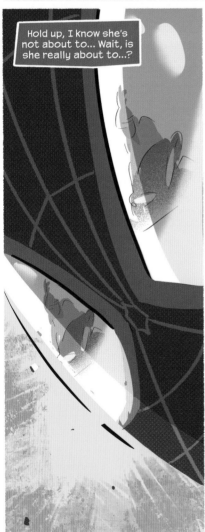

Nighty night, Spider-Man! Be safe out here!

Oh, c'mon. Can I catch a break? Just one?

Okay, you got this. Being a super hero is about adjusting on the fly.

Sooo, let's adjust.

Hey, you're gonna wanna make this next right, and the precinct will be on our left.

Sorry, man, but this isn't a ride-share.

29

32

"Sorry, I was busy trying not to be captured. Besides, you can just purple teleport us back to grab it."

THJUMP!

OOOOF!

"If we lose that bag, Vex, I swear..."

I don't get it. This hot dog cart is s'posed to be the red-train entrance.

Oh wow, B-R-B! I'll die if I don't get a pic with Spidey!

O-M-G, can you imagine if we saw the *real* Spider-Man here? I'd lose my whole mind...

Hmph. I wouldn't shell out twenty bucks for the *real* Spider-Man...

Umm, Trinity, how's that teleport situation looking?!

What do you think I'm trying to *do*?

34

CHAPTER
THREE

MR. MORALES!

Huh, what, here, in attendance, please no more tea!

HA HA HA HA HA HA HA HA HA HA HA HA HA HA HA HA HA HA HA

Bro, you can't jack my nightmares.

You just earned yourself detention, Mr. Morales.

A few minutes later.

So, S.I. stands for Serval Industries?

One hundred percent.

And you know this how?

Because my dad works at Serval and he has the same stone, only smaller.

So your dad's a scientist?

Maybe he can tell us why someone would wanna steal this thing.

Maybe. But he's a security analyst, not a scientist. Which is why I thought it was weird when I saw him carrying it everywhere. I ran a few scans through this petrology app that I built in summer camp, but I couldn't find a match.

Petrology?

The study of rocks. Keep up, bro. And wait, you build apps, Kyle?

All the time. Tech is life.

Plus, my dad has dreams of me following in his engineering foot-steps, so...

Hate to interrupt you two rock lovers, but any chance you could call your dad and ask him about the rock, Kyle?

Maybe, but first I have two questions.

One, where'd you get your rock from? And two, why do you care so much about it?

Oh, she's gooooood.

One, I found it on the street. And two, I've got a thing for rocks.

Common room, later that evening.

Kyle's right. I did a deep search and I can't find a single thing about our new pet rock.

I thought you and Kyle were supposed to be computer experts.

tap tap tap

Really, bro? You're throwing shade after all the *free tech* I've done for you?

Dad, this is Kyle again. I know you're probably working late, but hit me back as soon as you can, *please.*

Love you.

tap tap tap

This isn't like him. Something's wrong.

When was the last time you heard from him?

He texted me a few hours ago.

And what did he say?

Nothing. The text was meant for someone named Tara Jean.

One of your dad's co-workers maybe?

No clue.

Tap tap

Okay, but what was the *exact* message?

44

Hey, thanks again for this Cloud-9 ice cream, Tara Jean. But it's a little metallic-y.

I think this is good news.

What do you mean?

If your dad was somehow in trouble, he wouldn't have been able to text you a few hours ago.

And if he were in trouble but had his phone, he could've just called the police or your mom or told you exactly what was happening to him, right?

I mean, I guess.

Plus, your mom said she thinks he'll turn up at home any minute.

But this isn't like him. Whenever he works late, he still calls me at 8:00PM It was the same back in Cleveland. Always 8:00PM, no matter what.

Well, it's nearly 9:30 now, so...

And I'm not helping, am I? Really sorry. I think my sugar's low. Gonna grab a snack. You guys want?

I can't stomach anything right now, but thanks.

I'm good, man.

Hey, I meant to ask you, that technique you were using in art, where you were crosshatching the—

Hey, if it's cool with you, maybe we can talk about art another time?

Oh. Yeah. I just thought maybe you could use a distraction and—

A distraction from worrying about my dad?

That's... interesting.

Oh wow. No, I didn't mean it like *that.*

Until I hear from my dad, I'm not gonna be able to think about anything else.

Okay, sure, that makes sense. I was just trying to help.

Honestly, I probably shouldn't have involved you, anyway. We just met. We don't even know each other.

I mean, fair, but that doesn't mean I don't care about your dad.

You know what? We should call it a night. I'm suddenly very tired.

Kyle, wait. I'm sorry I—

No, it's cool. I'll see you around. Night.

SLAM!

CHOOMP CHOOMP CHOONM'PP

So, that went well.

How did I miss Mom's calls? Shoot, it's too late to call her back now.

And I didn't mean to make Kyle mad. I thought a distraction would help her.

Okay, maybe I was also hoping she could help pull me outta my art slump.

It's like I'm being dragged in every direction. And now I can't do anything right.

47

YAWWNN

ZOOP-ZOOP

MAMÍ

Missed you last night. Meet me for lunch at the deli on the corner. Already cleared it with your school. Love, Mom.

SCHHUUP

All right, Miles. Be cool.

Uhhh, hey, Kyle, what's up... Hey, Kyle, good, uh, morning. Sorry about last—

Listen to me, Kyle.

I know you're scared. But it's gonna be okay.

Something bad's happened. I can feel it.

You know your father, how he gets so caught up in his work... He'll turn up any minute now and then we'll tag team him for making us worry.

Then how come his boss, Mr. Snow, said he saw Dad leave work yesterday at 6:00PM?

Hey, sorry to interrupt, and I know you probably don't wanna talk to me right now, but...

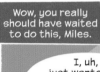

Wow, you really should have waited to do this, Miles.

I, uh, just wanted to apologize for, uh, last night. I shouldn't have—

Wow, you really have the worst timing.

I told you— you should've waited.

Kyle, I—

Kyle, where are you going?

Maybe you two can form a dismiss all of Kyle's concerns club. But something's happened to my dad, and I'm gonna find out what.

A few moments later.

Okay, so this Mr. Granderson was last seen leaving work at 6:00 p.m.? You got an employer name?

Mr. Snow. At Serval Industries, I think.

Wait, Harrison Snow? As in one of the wealthiest, most powerful people on the planet? Talk about coincidences...

What's the coincidence?

Snow's here.

What do you mean *here*?

Those are two of his "most promising" interns, ha. Snow says he rescued them from the streets. Claims he's helping them make something of themselves.

Yeah, two super-powered criminals.

Meanwhile, these two "success" stories damaged a million dollars in property last night. Officers and civilians were injured too.

So how come they're *leaving* jail?

The chief ordered their release. Says we're lucky Mr. Snow's not filing charges against us.

But one thing I know is that the good or bad you do in this world eventually comes back to you... Which reminds me, you missed the fundraiser meeting last night.

Oh shoot. That explains Mom's lunch invite.

Son, I know you have obligations at that school, but...this means a lot to Mom and to me.

Miles? Miles, are you hearing me?

Before you say anything, I'm so sorry I missed the meeting. A friend was having some trouble, and I—

It's fine, mijo.

ABBY'S DELI

Burger and fries, my favorite. Thanks, Mom. So how was the meeting?

Great. People are really stepping up.

That's awesome.

There was a little girl begging her dad to chase her around the meeting room. So cute. Reminded me of Papa chasing me around our yard, ha. He—

Miles?

52

ZZZZZZZ MILES!

SLAAAAT

I said **no tea!** Huh? Dang it, I did it again.

That right there, that's exactly what I'm afraid will happen with this earthquake.

That people will smoosh their burgers?

No, that people will grow tired and bored. That the earthquake will be old news and it'll be years before Puerto Rico recovers.

We're not gonna let that happen, Mom. I promise.

You promise? Miles, you can't even stay awake for five minutes.

I'm sorry, Mom. I've just been stressed, and th—

What was more important than supporting your mother last night? Supporting your family and friends? Our culture?

Mom, I'm... There's nothing more important. I just... I got mixed up, and—

Seems to me your priorities are the only things mixed up.

Later that evening.

Thanks for meeting me, man.

Sorry I don't have a lot of time, but I've been out all day, and MJ will kill me if I'm late for dinner.

Nah, don't sweat it. I was just hoping for some advice...

I told you, eventually you'll get used to how tight the costume is...

Hahaha.

I'm sorry. Continue.

I guess what I want to know is...like... how do you balance it all? Being a super hero versus being present for your family and friends?

I know how you're feeling.

Honestly, I'm still trying to figure that out.

But listen, super heroes make mistakes too. We get distracted like anyone else. But when we find ourselves drifting, the important thing is to get back on track.

But how?

Sometimes it might mean apologizing to someone we've let down.

Sometimes it means something as simple as not being late to dinner.

Which is why I gotta hustle, man.

I appreciate you meeting me out here.

Anytime, brother. You know that.

And I know Arbitration Rock ain't much to look at, but, I don't know, the two of us being here feels right.

Yep, even though this rock isn't actually the border between Brooklyn and Queens anymore...

...It's where our boroughs come together.

Oh wow, it's Serval Industries.

Snow definitely spared no expense. And this view is sick.

Looks like someone's working late.

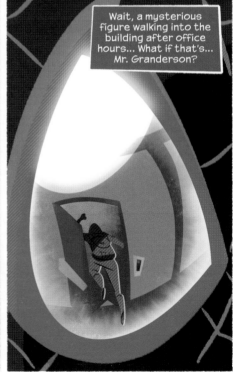

Wait, a mysterious figure walking into the building after office hours... What if that's... Mr. Granderson?

56

Now, which way did our mysterious friend go—

BINGG

This is too easy.

Third floor, cool. I think I'll take the stairs though.

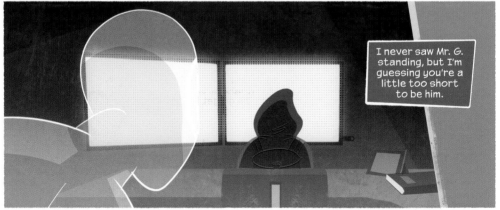

I never saw Mr. G. standing, but I'm guessing you're a little too short to be him.

My bad. I'm new here, so...

And what were you doing in Mr. Granderson's office?

I was shadowing him for my internship. I thought I left my notebook here, but I was wrong.

Jennifer, what's your last name? I gotta call this in and verify you're allowed to be here after hours.

Wait, is Whitney hyphenated, or is that your middle na—

No problem. Jennifer Whitney Ejiofor.

Hyphenated! Be right back!

John, where are you? We may have a situation here. Over.

I'm on the pot, Larry. Either you handle it, or it's gonna have to wait a minute. Over.

Hey, don't worry, man. I'm on it.

What the—?! Who's there? John, you pranking me again?!

CHIME!

What in the world was that?

I'm almost off the pot, Larry. Everything under control? Over.

Don't worry, Larry. I'll know how to find her.

CHAPTER

FOUR

Back to the drawing board, huh? Hahaha. How's the winning art contest submission coming along?

I've heard of writer's block. Who knew there was an artist's block too?

You'll find your way, bro. I believe in you.

That makes one of us.

Kyle's not answering my texts. I hope she's okay. I hope her dad's okay.

Yeah, maybe you should get to class early so you can talk to her.

Tracker back up yet?

Bro. Stop.

KYLE

Hey, sorry to text you again, but just worried about you.

Missed you in class today. Hope everything's okay.

"...in our school library."

GPS doesn't lie.

You sure you don't need me to go with?

No, this is the only way in or out. If I lose them, they'll have to walk by you. Then you can—

Take them down!

No. You can get a good look at them.

Dude, what if the thief's one of our teachers? What if it's Mrs. Cloverfield? Then you can give her detention, ha!

Yeah, the detention *center*. Haha. Get it? As in prison?

Bro, I got it. Just wasn't that funny.

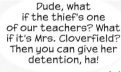

Whatever. See you in a few.

Take your time. I'll just be here...by myself... waiting for bad guys...

69

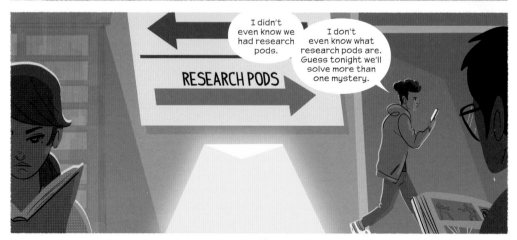

RESEARCH PODS

RESEARCH PODS

Looks like we have *two* contestants for **WHO BROKE INTO SERVAL** last night.

Let's meet our first contestant.

Okay, unless you grew three feet overnight, you are *not* our fake intern.

Which means it has to be...

Oh, c'mon. Are you serious?

This is unbelievable. I *really* can't catch a break.

Excuse me! What do you think you're doing?

Oh, it's you. Sorry. Forgot my hoodie.

Wait, what?! Kyle's the burglar?

Missed you in class. Your roomie said you were out late last night. Was it about your dad?

Huh? Oh no. I was...running an errand. Dad's still... missing.

I'm so sorry you're—

No, I'm sorry. You wanted to help, and I pushed you away. It's just hard not knowing if he's okay.

I want you to know that, uh... I got you, Kyle. Ganke does too. And my dad's a police officer, and he wants to help too.

I don't know what to say. Thank you, Miles.

Kyle...yesterday when I met your mom, you said you were gonna find out what happened to your dad?

Yeah, and?

If something *has* happened to your dad, it could be dangerous.

I'm not afraid, and I *don't* need your protection.

I know. All I'm saying is sometimes when we're desperate for answers, we take risks that could—

I'd risk *everything* to find my dad.

Even if it means your mom loses you too?

RECEPTION

72

Wow. For real?

My dad said that last night a young Black female with computer skills broke into Serval.

Okay, wait. Are you accusing me?

Kyle, your dad wouldn't want you to—

You don't know my dad, Miles! And you don't know me!

If you found a clue that could lead to your dad, we should tell the police. My dad—

Later, Morales.

Bro, we're s'posed to be all *To Catch a Thief* out here, but you're too busy getting caught up with Kyle?!

One, I was doing **both**. And two, you finally watched it?! Cary Grant's dope, right?

Miles, focus, man! Where's our burglar?!

73

Okay,
but why would
Kyle break into
Serval?

Maybe
it's what
they might
lose.

Because
she's searching
for her dad.

So she
thinks Serval
disappeared her dad?
Why? What would
they gain?

One day I'd
love to discuss
the fact that you
get to do all the
fun stuff.

Aww, Ganke,
I'd be lost without
your awesome
techie brain.

THWIPP

You're
just saying
that.

This
tracking
app that you
recalibrated
is pretty
dope.

Actually,
I completely
redesigned
it.

See? You're
a tech god. But,
uh, looks like Kyle's
on the move,
so.

Text me
when you're on
your way home?
I worry.

Gotcha.

And 0 for two. Obviously, I need to chill on the rhetorical questions...

KLICK

Back so soon?

Who's there?

Just your friendly neighborhood Spider-Man. And you are?

ALL LAB DELIVERIES HERE

Spider-Man.

No, that's me. Who are you, and why are you breaking into Serval?

I...I have urgent business here.

I can't let you go in there.

I wasn't asking permission.

THWAAAAP

Sorry, that door's out of order tonight.

What do you think you're doing?!

Weird, but I have the **exact same** question for you.

My dad works here. **I'm allowed** to be here. **You** on the other hand... Please don't make me go full Karen and call security.

Definitely call security. They're gonna **love** your illegal door unlocking program.

Dad was right. The second person always gets caught.

What does that mean?

It's a sports thing. One player shoves an opponent and gets away with it, but as soon as the opponent retaliates, the whistle blows.

Okay, I need a little more...

It means you're preventing me from breaking in because you wanna uphold the law, which, fine. Except I only want in because **they** did something to my dad first.

ALL
DELIV
H

And you have evidence of this not-good something?

We're losing time! Every second matters!

Do you have **evidence,** Kyle?

Whoa, nuh-uh, what are you doing?!

Helping you break down years of unresolved trust issues through increased vulnerability via a sudden and unexpected revealing of your true identity?

Sooo, Mom's a therapist.

Ahh, makes sense. But there will be no unmasking tonight, thanks.

Yeah, I'm sorry. It felt like a moment.

Kyle, if you have any info that might help us find your dad, now's the time to share.

You never answered. How do you know my name?

Your backpack. Front pocket.

Well, that's anticlimactic.

KYLE ANDERSON

=Sigh= Okay, so before my dad disappeared, he sent me a text.

tap
tap
tap

And this text said, "Help, there's something bad happening at Serval"?

Nope. It said, "Hey, thanks again for this Cloud-9 ice cream, Tara Jean. But it's a little metallic-y."

Okay, so your dad loves the frozen metal-tasting dairy that someone named Tara Jean gave him.

At first I figured he texted me when he meant to text this Tara Jean person. No big deal. But then I thought maybe Tara Jean knows something.

What did she say?

Nothing. Because she doesn't exist.

I don't follow.

I checked Dad's contacts **and** used his office computer to access Serval's employee database. There is no Tara Jean. So either Dad made a typo or...

He was texting you in code.

tap *tap*
tap
tap

Watch.

80

CHAPTER
FIVE

Turns out it was auto-uploaded onto my private storage account—Cloud 9.

So your dad was walking around with a camera glued to his shirt and no one noticed?

This was the only video uploaded, so I'm guessing it was the only time he wore it.

He must've been worried something might happen to him.

Yep. And no one would've realized it was a camera because...

...to anyone else it's a silly lapel pin that your wannabe spy daughter begged you to buy for making honor roll.

FUN TECH FOR KIDS!
SECRET "SPY" CAMERA FOR YOUR ICE CREAM LOVING KID!

Like your dad's text. *Metallic-y ice cream.* But what about *Tara Jean?*

That's the only part of the code I don't understand.

SECRET "SPY" CAMERA FOR YOUR ICE CREAM LOVING KID!

Kyle, the police need to see this.

The police can't stop Snow in time. But *we* can.

Oui? Oh, you speak French now?

tap

Who are you calling? The police?

No. Two good friends actually.

84

Wait, why are you calling? Was Avengers Academy today? Did I miss it?

No, I need your help with a code.

You know we love *code-breaking.* What's up?

A few moments later.

Wow, you've had a busy week.

Tell me about it.

Well, I just ran a search cross-referencing Tara Jean and Serval, and... there's nothing here.

Guys, maybe we're approaching this all wrong. What if Tara Jean isn't a woman? Or even a person?

Okay, so Tara Jean's a... *thing?*

Those two girls working with Snow, Trinity and Vex? They were normal the first time you saw them, right? But then, suddenly, they had powers?

Yep.

And there's some weird rock that everyone wants except you can't identify it, right?

OMG, that's it! Kamala, you're a *rock* star! Pun intended.

You would've figured it out too!

We make a great team!!!

Umm, hello, anyone wanna explain to me what we're so excited about?

So this missing dad was pretty clever. Tara Jean is actually code for...

...Terrigen!

Didn't we learn about Terrigen Crystals at the academy, like, a while back?

Yep. Basically, Terrigen Crystals create a Terrigen Mist. When Inhumans are exposed to this mist—

Wait, Inhumans— aren't they the result of long-ago alien experiments, which made them superhuman, right?

SERVAL INDUSTRIES

Essentially, yes. Except their descendants are not born superhuman. That's where the mist comes in.

Exposure to Terrigen Mist triggers a reaction in Inhumans called Terrigenesis—which generates super-powers and abilities.

Okay, but what happens when people who don't carry the Inhuman gene are exposed to the Terrigen Mist?

I can't believe I'm doing this... What's your number?

Why?

I'll call you if...I don't know... I need backup or whatever.

You're not gonna call. You're just trying to get rid of me.

Look, it's this or I glue you to the wall with webbing.

Call me!

So the Terrigen Crystals explain Trinity's and Vex's new powers. But what if they're only the beginning?

Snow could use the Terrigen to build an entire super-army. Based on that video, world peace isn't his mission statement.

STAIRWELL A

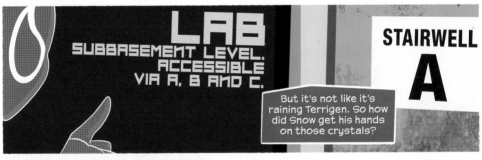

LAB
SUBBASEMENT LEVEL.
ACCESSIBLE
VIA A, B AND C.

STAIRWELL
A

But it's not like it's raining Terrigen. So how did Snow get his hands on those crystals?

LAB →

I think it's time I ask Snow myself.

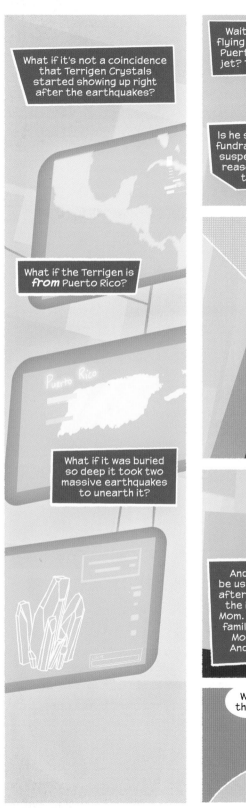

What if it's not a coincidence that Terrigen Crystals started showing up right after the earthquakes?

What if the Terrigen is *from* Puerto Rico?

What if it was buried so deep it took two massive earthquakes to unearth it?

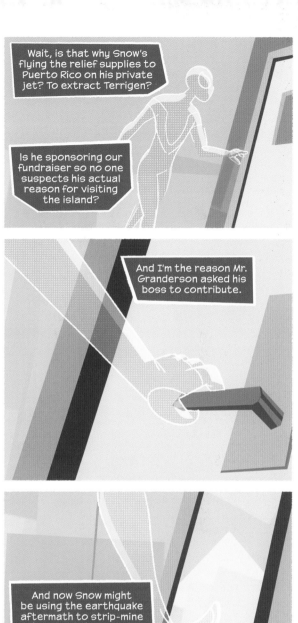

Wait, is that why Snow's flying the relief supplies to Puerto Rico on his private jet? To extract Terrigen?

Is he sponsoring our fundraiser so no one suspects his actual reason for visiting the island?

And I'm the reason Mr. Granderson asked his boss to contribute.

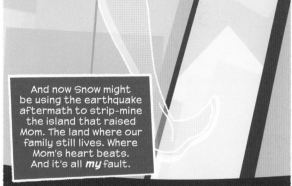

And now Snow might be using the earthquake aftermath to strip-mine the island that raised Mom. The land where our family still lives. Where Mom's heart beats. And it's all *my* fault.

What the—?!

For future reference, a nonautomatic door opening on its own? Dead giveaway.

Noted.

Sorry, Spider-Man, I've got a chopper to catch. But my top two interns are happy to entertain you.

No one comes between me and my friend, Spider-Man.

BAVOOOOOSH

PING

Apparently Snow designed this building to last. Makes sense when you expect to have a lot of super-powered people hanging around.

KLONG

THWIPP

Anyone ever tell you your aim stinks?

Oof, this thing weighs a ton.

You're really doing the blast thing again? Your last shot nearly took you out.

Ha, guess I'm hardheaded.

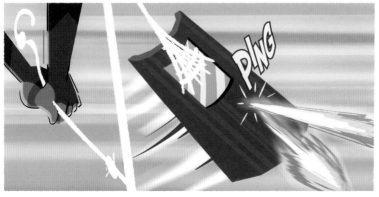

PING

Guess not hardheaded enough.

Impressive, Spider-Man. But you're far too late.

What do you want with Puerto Rico?

96

And where's Mr. Granderson?

C'mon, you know the answer to your first question. But not to worry, I'm making a *very* generous donation to their relief efforts.

As for my favorite security analyst, well, he's right beside you.

I wouldn't disturb him if I were you. The transmutation process can be quite volatile. I'd hoped to take him with me. Unfortunately...

...he's not quite finished yet.

CHAPTER
SIX

It can't be. He's just an ordinary human.

Ha, turns out Mr. Cliff's anything but.

Let's continue this discussion face-to-face, Snow.

Actually, Spider-Man, you're going to stay there. Unless you want to see if your friend can fly.

Spider-Man, just help my dad!

Let her go **now** or I'll dedicate every day of my life to making yours miserable.

Big talk from a small bug. It's simple. You stay away, she lives. But interfere with my Terrigen acquisition and she's dead.

You're not getting the Terrigen.

Ha, I admire your—

Spider-Man, gooooooo!

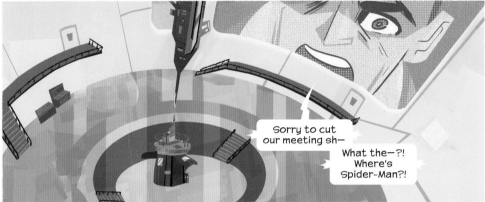

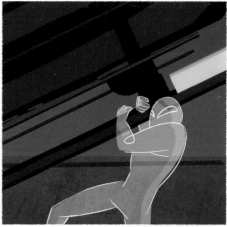

That blasted Spider-Man's got us tethered! Crank us up to full power! It's the only way we'll break free from—

This isn't good.

NOOOOOOO!

Please tell me you know how to fly this thing.

Sorry, this flight's been canceled due to bad Snow fall.

Groan.

Sure you can't let him just fall?

Kyle.

Fine. At least scare him a bit.

THWIPP

SERVAL INDUSTRIES

Mom, there's something I need to tell you. Dad... He's...

"It's okay, Kyle. No matter what happens, we're still a family and he's still your father."

WHSHHHH

"Nothing can change that."

But the resilient people of Puerto Rico are working hard to rebuild their communities, and they are confident that soon this island will thrive yet again. This is Lauren Cait, reporting live from Puerto Rico.

Thanks, Lauren. Meanwhile, in breaking news, Harrison Snow, famed CEO of Serval Industries, is in police custody. We'll have more on that at the top of the hour.

Oh man, it's almost 6:00— I better get going!

Sorry I'm late!

No, mijo, you're right on time.

106

I'm so happy so many want to be involved.

All of that organizing made me hungry. Should we grab dinner?

Actually, I was hoping we could do family dinner at home.

BROOKLYN COMMUNITY CENTER

Mijo, what's gotten into you? We should drop you off back at school so you can do your homework.

Nah. Homework can wait. Some things are more important.

Oh, mijo.

...and you should've seen your abuela's face when she saw how high I'd climbed up that tree. But then she started climbing too, laughing all the way up.

Later...

...but your dad was afraid of Papa.

Not afraid. **Respectful.** And okay, your dad's a **little** imposing.

So your dad asked Papa and Abuela if we could all walk through the El Yunque rain forest.

Whaaat?! Dad, you hate nature!

I hate **mosquitoes.** I love nature.

The real reason is he knew Papa wouldn't say no because Abuela loves the rain forest more than any place.

Later still...

I love your stories, Mom. It's like I'm there on the island with you.

You know, I was afraid no one would show at the meeting today.

But this community rallying in support of the land that raised me, it's beautiful.

But this time with my son and my husband, my family... **This** is the best part of my day.

107

The Serval spokesperson just emailed that the fundraiser still has their full support and said, "Snow's inexcusable actions are not what their company stands for."

I bet, Rio. Pretty sure Serval's looking for all the good press it can get right now.

WITH LOVE, FROM EL YUNQUE

My dearest Miles,

Just a small note to let you know we're thinking of you always and can't wait to take you to one of our favorite places in all of the island—El Yunque!

We miss you.

Love,
Abuela

Maybe I've been approaching this art thing all wrong. Maybe instead of just focusing on **how** I'm drawing, I should think about **why** I'm drawing.

What if my art represented the stories that have shaped my life? The stories of my family's life?

What if I create with my mind and my heart?

The next morning.

Hey, Kyle, I heard about... I can't imagine how you feel, but our family is here for yours.

He's still not awake, but the doctors are hopeful. The hardest part is waiting. I could use a distraction.

"Wanna go for a walk?"

Wow.

You could do that. Your art is fire, K.

Plus, I...uhh, wait. Why didn't I think of this before?

Think of what?

A few blocks farther.

JUSTIN'S JAMS

This.

I'm in, but only if we do this together.

I hope I don't regret this, but okay, my answer is yes.

The day of the fundraiser.

...and Serval is proud to announce we are **tripling** our donation toward the relief efforts, in our support of the great people of Puerto Rico.

Your fundraiser app is a big hit.

Was there ever any doubt?

Our head judge, Abe, is set to announce our art contest winners!

A few moments later.

Moment of truth, bro. You nervous?

Nah. No matter what, I'm happy with how it turned out.

And finally, our grand prize art contest winners are... Kyle Granderson and Miles Morales!

Dad, this is for you...

"Get better soon!"

JUSTIN A. REYNOLDS has always wanted to be a writer. *Opposite of Always*, his debut novel, was an Indies Introduce selection and a School Library Journal Best Book, has been translated into seventeen languages and is being developed for film with Paramount Players. His second novel, *Early Departures*, arrived September 2020. Justin hangs out in northeast Ohio with his family and likes it and is probably somewhere, right now, dancing terribly. You can find him at justinareynolds.com.

PABLO LEON is an artist and designer whose clients include Warner Brothers Animation, OddBot Inc., Puny Entertainment, Bento Box Entertainment, and more. His original comic story *The Journey*, about the true accounts of people migrating from Latin America to the United States, was a 2019 Eisner Award nominee. He lives in Los Angeles, California.

CHECK OUT A SNEAK PEEK OF

MS. MARVEL
STRETCHED THIN

COMING **FALL 2021!**

WRITTEN BY
NADIA SHAMMAS

ILLUSTRATED BY
NABI H. ALI

LAYOUTS BY
GEOFFO

LETTERS BY
VC's JOE CARAMAGNA

Kamala?

Kamala! Nakia is waiting for you!

Ughhhhh... I'm uuuuup...

KAMALA!!! YOU ARE GOING TO BE LATE!!!

I'm up! I'm up! I'm com—

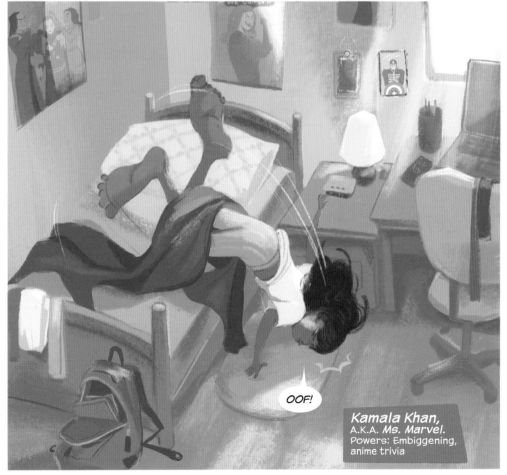

OOF!

Kamala Khan,
A.K.A. *Ms. Marvel.*
Powers: Embiggening, anime trivia

Nakia, A.K.A. Kiki.
(But don't call her that.)
Powers: Critical thinking,
podcast recommendations

Kamala, that is some "pull yourself up by your bootstraps" capitalist nonsense.

The Terrigen Mist happened just a few months ago, so you've had your powers for less than a year. Meaning you've been Ms. Marvel less than a *year*. You're doing great, but it's okay to be tired.

I'm not tired. I've just...got a lot on my plate. But it's fine! Looking forward to a day at school.

I mean...you look pretty tired.

I'm not!

Mm...please, Donald Duck... we need your keyblade to beat this Black Souls boss...

Wake up, Ms. I'm-Not-Tired.

I'm not tired... Just this one class...

This is the last class of the day. You fell asleep in every class.

Last class of the day...

Last class of the day!

Hey, Kamala, you coming to the computer lab today? I've been working on—

Sorry, I've got ten minutes to pick up Malik from daycare and then get to training! Next time!!!

Yeah... Next time...

Thanks, Lauren! Great to see you again, gottagobye!!!

Bye, Kamala...?